SIDEBROW BOOKS

FIELD GLASS

Published by Sidebrow Books
P.O. Box 86921
Portland, OR 97286
sidebrow@sidebrow.net
www.sidebrow.net

Cover art by Brian Mashburn
Cover & book design by Jason Snyder

ISBN: 1-940090-06-7
ISBN-13: 978-1-940090-06-1

FIRST EDITION | FIRST PRINTING
9 8 7 6 5 4 3 2 1
SIDEBROW BOOKS 017
PRINTED IN THE UNITED STATES

Sidebrow Books titles are distributed by
Small Press Distribution

Titles are available directly from Sidebrow at
www.sidebrow.net/books

A Member of

www.theintersection.org

Sidebrow is a member of the Intersection Incubator, a program of
Intersection for the Arts (www.theintersection.org) providing fiscal
sponsorship, incubation, and consulting for artists. Contributions
to Sidebrow are tax-deductible to the extent allowed by law.

FIELD GLASS

JOANNA HOWARD & JOANNA RUOCCO

SIDEBROW BOOKS + 2017 + PORTLAND & SAN FRANCISCO

'Eliminating distance kills,' Rene Char once said. When you endlessly increase the liberating power of the media, you bring what once was hidden by distance and the secret—which was distant and naturally foreign to each one of us—far too close; you then run the risk of reinventing, here and now, some kind of *barbarism* (*barbaros* = foreigner, one who does not speak the language). In other words, you run the risk of *inventing the enemy.*

—Paul Virilio

There the insurgents made their soundless lair. Openings in the hedgerow were closed with frames made from the same material as the hedge. The occupied could close the leafy door, slip into fields and forest, and leave no trace of passing. On a sunny day a deserter could walk for hours and emerge from the bocage as pale as a spirit.

Those who took to the fields hovered, sheltered, burrowed in open space, or insurgents kept off the advancing ranks by throwing stones. A fox hunt has been going on for some time—human foxes and a motorized hunt. In compounds, in reserves, in a mall of houses, the occupied observe the war as if through soda lime, as if through a liquid state.

Drive on, despite the broken bridge. It means a detour of about ten miles over practically impassable footpaths, the last mile through the bed of a stream, heavy vehicles waterlogged and discarded. Darkness, streets in ruins in rivulets; strewn with shells, fine chalk dust suspended in the air. Wander through the labyrinth of corridors and courtyards.

The colporteur lies in the wallow, neck broken, surrounded by maps of the territories. That wallow was deeper once: a trench in the time of occupation. Water collected. The colporteur is half-mud himself, rotten as his maps. Here and there, the spines of books. Roots or chewed leather. Gelatin and silver. How many meters of plastic tape—unspooled—tangle now in thorns?

In that time, the houses were behind the hedgerows, beyond the trenches, obscured in the middle realm between the landings and the stations, that forest that was a town that was an outpost. Is it resistance if disguised as trees? When the forest exploded, there stood revealed a swarming mass of men. Then they stood no longer.

Of those who received a signal—a warning felt as static in the air or a hertz disturbing rhythms in the heart—and ran, some shapes remain, printed on the macadam in ash. Of those who received before even this forewarning a secret missive (inscribed on the molar of a rat; spelled with vapors in the air by drones controlled remotely), a love poem or ultimatum, a timetable of the patrols, a key to the bunkers (inside the fake oak, the bark of which, a rolled layer of corking, is marked by four ax strokes; along the stubble, beneath the third windrow from the combine with the feeder throat cut to half its length and leaking sorghum; up the ladder of the gantry crane; between the mitre gates in the dry canal; at the lock-keeper's house, he is a friend; at the Consul's house, he is a traitor) and tiptoed away in advance of every fire, nothing remains. They attained or they evaporated.

Event dispatches outgoing to partitions, but beyond partitions? Communiqués moved through the cluster connection, in a round-robin, though no external events relayed back in sequence. Spooling and releasing, or collected to a central frame, an output overflow, transmission to a control pylon, to the panopticon? Where data is no longer "given" but is certainly collated? It is uncertain. Lingual scrap.

Ringing the colporteur's oddly angled head, a few yellow teeth but the dark runnels are wormholes and no message can be read. Inspected through the glass, worms passing through that dark perform a glottic writing. Decrease the distance. The parts of these letters subtend what angle at the eye? Refractive error or an error in the object. There is no corrective. The encryption is absolute.

The house exists, nothing but a charcoal kiln. The walls, sheets frozen on the lines. There's no wind. Each tree is the base of a stairway. The countryside here is so provincial. The cats are all virgins. I've gotten sick of watching birds bathe, of acknowledging the women who walk alongside paths according to their custom. Raised palms, a slight bow. I stopped one for conversation. She gave my greeting back to me—"Cold day. It is. It is a cold day. It is a cold day. It is. It is. A cold day"—and would not walk on. She's still standing there. Our only hope: she grows into the tree line. It was a cold day, a very cold day. I won't go out in it again.

[outstream]

We gather the juice of the common kinds—dog's tooth, knotgrass, coral wort—to be boiled in wine. Conditions fritter away in our gamble. Ivor jokes, his peculiar mode of feeling. A survivor of the maladies, his subject is ascribed in the telling. I jot briefly, follow the thread.

[outstream]

What brought us here drives us out, but we remain. No more bread! Snows, and bitten by venomous creatures. The executioner lies unknown, and all jurisdiction is mere tactics. Home has lost its command. There must be a better way to interlocute? Fine, then, I'll do the job myself.

The kindling box is heaped with pieces of loose
literature: *Gringoire*, revue of the liberate world,
silence notebooks, *The Workman's Tradewinds*.
Pre-war weeklies of virulent turn. I can sit for
hours engaged in piecework. Fingers feed.

[outstream]

Don't linger, handsome eyes, by the highway sides, footpaths, hornet's nest where knotgrass grows. Time seen as an image is time lost, a drifting wreckage, like the shipbuilders I recall from childhood. Shipwreckers more like. Second fiddle to clocks, no longer! Hourglass into lion's paw. Daredevils. We dismount our vehicle. We inject a corrupting influence into these meadows, could they be described as such. The manhunt begins.

[spool release]

Our mood is incurable. I wait to be relieved of it, like an animal in milk, until each day is shorter than the one that comes after. I've never understood the ratios. All I know for certain is our position has not changed. The house is squared to the barn, the barn to the corn crib. We eat, smoke, drink but never visibly. As far as Ivor knows we're motionless and unadorned: cornstalks unprepared to ear.

The snow is nocturnal. It broods inside the trees, comes out when the silence condenses on the darkened trunks. We tell stories around the centerpiece, roses in a pewter bowl. I speak directly to the mic in the corolla. I remember an attack at dawn, the sun above the waves, and on the shore an entire army that keeled over into dunes of shamming dead. A few soldiers dressed as ghosts, in residues, roamed bewildered in the surf or pushed sand above the tidal line into scarps and trenches sized for a general's model or child's game. I am suggesting something similar. For example, all the bullets have grown a moss. The fish and sherry never quarrel. Here comes a cantaloupe escorted by a ripe Sauterne.

[outstream]

This year we've grown grain so bright that it frightens the beasts like fire. We scythed in masks, long-sleeves, and gloves (my idea). Mice won't approach the silage. The squirrels fill the pines on the perimeter. When you described the moon in terms of sage and tin, I stopped reading. I don't look for your letters. I really think you are no longer capable of dying. It makes me love these hectares, our inheritance, more violently. I won't sleep. I will even cultivate the weeds.

[spool release]

Ivor says all is well here. I believe him.

[outstream]

Here is the signaling medium: on-off, as long as the electricity holds, I will continue to report. I welcome the buzz of it, but Ivor is sensitive from overexposure and feels it in parts of himself where he ought not. Let no woman be too busy with it, he tells me, it works very violent upon the feminine part. I say, on days when I believe in it, it drives off the venomous serpents. He grins out from the crib, where he squats in the husking to collect himself, and protect his thoughts. My spirits oscillate, as no doubt you will detect.

[outstream]

Fact: uprootedness occurs, particularly in time of occupation. And the urge is simply to uproot others. We are under the sign of silence, enemies lodged in neighboring chambers, bugs under hotel beds, hoary leaves set at a joint, but the observer sees different creatures. Stray voltage, wire tap, backflow of current, magnetic field. I am undaunted and will not belabor the code, but it seeks you for the moment by spark gap. Ivor is willing to return to telegraphy, but I can't expose him yet in his current state. Likely a decoction of the calamint with salt and honey will worm him, and provoke sweat.

[outstream]

I am thinking of us. Ourself as a presence which continues, of objects and people we've clutched, incorporate selves. Is there a personal imperative dwelling deep inside us? We grow on heaths, uplands. There is a vague layer of thoughts which originates from our center person, but is there a barrier which encloses this? If so, it appears to be skin. Other beings are well outside this. It must be a thick barrier.

Noted herein—event log. The first operation as follows: create for ourselves a field that can be surveyed. Localize an invariant. Ivor chooses his eye, the executioner his thumb, the caretaker her footed glass, the one from which she sips her flips and fizzes. I wait for nightfall and, in the darkness, pick through broken seed heads. Exhausted, I lie like a toad beneath the harrow. If the enemy came I would ask to be hulled. What motivates the horizon's outsize moon? Ivor has become a country deb, measuring tapes around his waist and thigh, mouth filled with pins, a girl who seeks truth in diameter. The world persists. Too insidious. It can't be done away with.

[spool release]

The men I see from the window I judge to be real men, though hats and coats might hide their wax or bisque or springs. They speak fugitive cant, terms of local convenience, proper names. What I jot down doesn't last. They aren't those kinds of words. Nonetheless, I want some token. The caretaker is strict, allots sixteen to twenty inches per guest per table. We can't seat them all, the numberless majority. I would shout down to one man—the one in melton coat and trousers, the one whose hat blows off to disclose a charming, realistic face: blue eyes and dented chin—if only I could hone my voice, and aim it.

Another busy day positing objects. Ivor has one eye and sees just one of me. He says I can't know his loneliness, the longing he feels for doubled images. He reads me a poem about clawhammer mountains. Our house is composed of warm and cold shades, not haphazardly, and beyond the dooryard, barn, and field, there are certainly mountains. A forest horizon and an intervening blue. I see through distances and make associations easily. Poor Ivor. He is always between the figure and the ground. Some would say he does not exist. The electrocardiogram records rhythms, but he is pulseless, subjoined to our company like particle to verb.

There has always been the problem of communication systems. No less so in the beginning of this era of violent velocity. Several international symposia manifested little more than puzzles, mathematical in nature, with all the implications of rigor and magic that word entails. Laws enunciated, and eventual obstacles reduced to an explicable machine. It's a problem of data. Monitor, collect, collate, and redirect towards the current state, the current economy, the current mode of thinking. Conveyance not only of information and knowledge, but also error, opinion, orders, emotions, moods. Conveyance of heat and motion, also strength, weakness, and disease. Intelligence as geist, and as ballast, as fodder. And so the captives of misinformation dwelled in the occupation territories.

As with any place of dwelling, those who inhabit it learn to navigate its passages in the dark. Among the collectives, transmissions resist. It would be, after all, foolish to seek some elegant, simple, and useful scientific theory of running that would embrace runs of salmon and runs in hosiery? Into the dark passageway. Deliberately interior, as if to see and speak from inside a chimerical universe by choice! Not entirely without junction. Forms created by the absorption of other forms.

Swimming harbors or swarming arbors? French herbs or trench heros? Deceptive trails. Multiple marrows running in the bone, and three kinds of motion: magnitude, affection, place. Don't come to the desert if you are coming for the water.

Return upland. Paths marked by guides. Listen carefully. Text in archipelago. Objective accounts of certain figures divorced from the flow of their wider context. Points of reference both phonetic and thematic. Archipelagos of verbal fragment. Therein form constellations. A marriage face.

The little is all and the little occupies an enormous space.

Through fragment toward passage. A parallel destruction where the gesture and the instrument will always disappear one within the other. Asymmetry. Pulverisation. The natural world appears always through ellipses. And so a man bears evidence on his shoulders. A pleated script. The shoulder opened.

[outstream]

These sites like strongholds. Barn, field, crib, house, crib, field, barn. Deep bunkers vacated and bypassed. The world is not what I think, I tell myself, but what I live through. Misfortune invites misfortune and I won't fall prey. Last week, Ivor complained first of the tertian ague, then a spate of amnesia. I fed him root of the white lily that our great-grand Marguerite planted along an irregular perimeter a hundred years ago. Lilies are under the dominion of the moon, and can expel poisons, but their roots must first be bruised. Ivor spent an hour in the semblance of a corpse, but sprang alive almost as quickly, to return to his bustle. Ivor is beyond me as a creature, and seeks understanding from all ages simultaneously. Would that my limbic recollection was not made of wounds and wrongs.

[spool release]

Messages are passing. Via continuous wave, via semaphore and stereograph. Among women in travail, no less. We return to our roots of transmission, some dark and dismal fanaticism, trimly decked. Our age poisoned by currents, but we are of our age, and no better than our age. The caretaker catalogues the proclivities of the boarders. When ragtags appear at the edge of the wood, we take them for their measure. But all of us are deserters of one sort or another, and our crimes are many. Still, we will not do without our remaining finery, and we can make elegance of bits and tatters. The caretaker dressed the table this very day with a bouquet of cosmetic cabbages and purple artichokes, and I was reminded of the days of heliotrope pajamas and marmalade in silver, or so Ivor recounts by the gaslight, as it was once recounted to him.

Tweeze from the colporteur's skin the spiral filaments. They are hidden in the open, above the lip as the semblance of a long mustache. Continue on into the warren of exploded outbuildings. Count the boards, the stones. They were patterned by the utterance of bombs. There is no key. There are bed frames, chair legs, shutters. There are armatures of women posed standing and seated. Perhaps they were buttressed once with flesh and shawls and clogs. They were padded, strokable. Held baskets of flowers perfumed to smell living. Repeated greetings. Told stories. The time they traveled to a little bay. Such flaky fish and dancing on a patio. They said the names of their companions. I was jealous of Rosamund, her bloom. Sergio got down on one knee. His hands were so sweaty the ring shot over the railing and was lost in the water. Nigel found it, our hero. No, dear, it wasn't in the fish. What a fairy tale. In the mud, in the mud, he saw the gold glinting. A rose? For your sweetheart? Some have wads of fur inside, stoles or cats that sought shelter in the nests of wire. Bulky but each only a kilo of metal; one compaction truck could handle the lot. Push them against the wall. Sift for smaller items. Search the rubble for replacements of the plaintext. Then into the specimen bags, sort the paper tapes, the coding wheels and plug boards, patch cables and rings.

Next take note of all provender, of cutlery. Any curl of tin. Could they have gleaned? For morale most smoked instead of ate. One drum of soft potatoes. Crate of carrots. One hundred metal matchboxes containing intact matches: mildewed shanks, unignited phosphors. Razor blades. Glass, discs of metal, intact jars of tea, tobacco, red millet, white beans, bullet casings, thyme. Between broken pavements, ruts are worn around the radios. As many as the bones, that many more antennae. Areas of mulch, straw, and dung. What were the highs and lows of temperature? The weather is not autonomous. The sabotage was neither this nor that: not foreground. The backdrop disappeared. The sky came down.

In the courtyard, there are human bodies, smoke and sun cured, fluids pressed out, with sprocket holes around the edges. They can be pulled through the machine but the footage is skin—shades of black and red—flakes of charred meat, sometimes a paler flake that glistens. Frame by frame, degrading.

Enough within the walls. Go to the road. The road meanders, less road than river in its waveform. Why? No cause is evident except by reconstruction. The landscape without its history is made of guesswork and abstractions. What was a hill is now a flattened curve. The road follows its distortion. Best to go on foot. The tree line, upon close inspection, is not a line of trees. Transmission masts and receivers, thin as the thinnest saplings, rooted in concrete beneath baize carpet.

In the field beyond the cobbles, men's hats are mounded. Flat caps, stiff visors. Dark gloves and shoes. A jeep on its side from which boxes have tumbled, their equipment, shoddily packed. Oscilloscopes. Cathode ray screens. Circuits. Reels in cases. Loose tape. Splinters of plastic. Collect the spindles. During playback, the male voice is the audible false signal. When he says journeys end in lovers meeting, listen to the other layers. One is the explosion. The other is phonic, speech without words, a hiss that is human in origin, that persists in the ear when the tape turns off.

[outstream]

Surface rumblings, and then a noxious gas escapes the wellbore—the drilling goes deeper but comes closer. Through the hedge a cloud passes, an unknown color, an interior color. Some are now burrowing in, some are dropping. Soon the wells, as well, will burn venomous.

We have only the old seismograph to monitor the fractures, which I meet now with the regularity of the dawn. The last uncracked cup dropped its ear this morning, and so there are no more handles. No surprise. (No matter. Even the chicory is running out. The forage yields less: buds blanched, leaves dropping.) Now we meet the day with a flat grip on a broken exterior. No matter how hot, we cup it in the cup of the palms. Cup to cup, while the bitterness lasts. Luck that our limbs are numb in the tips and extremes, Ivor's and mine, an unexplained ailment. Possibly the cold, we say, or repeated exposures to scalding. Surely our mysteries define us.

[outstream]

Allow me this sentiment by special switch, by scrap of induction. It is hard not to recall that evening early on—my own one, wherever you are housed—under command of blackout with windows tarred and papered, and the mudroom absent of all light, we were seeking small parsnips for dinner among the slatted crates, and seizing what I thought to be a delectably sized item, I found that I had locked onto your very own warm finger. But you remained silent in your thoughts. Eyes in space? Ersatz! A figment of my own forgetting. Circuits hardwired in the stalk, we proceed by essences.

The caretaker used the pronouncing dictionary as a doorstop, but yesterday I picked it up and began to cultivate my voice. I never cared much for words themselves, just their pitches. Fondled children die young. Watch your mouth in the mirror while you read this. Always read aloud. Ivor read silently, alone, in private, and look! He grew a mustache, went half-blind and lost the eye. Now the door slams when the boarders use the toilet or go into the kitchen to heat tea. They needn't be so careless. Life is not made for that.

[outstream]

Even after I examined the landscape upside down for several hours, I couldn't convince myself that orientation was the obstacle. Dispirited, I left my post. I brought the kitchen radio into the barn. The damp bales were hot so I turned out my pockets and pressed apples deep inside to soften. I wished my teeth were better or else my lip—that it had a longer drape. Remember I had filled my head with blood. You once said I was an allusion to a general type. I said you were the middle term, that I saw you between God and nothing. You patted my cheek with your free hand; with the other you kept shading elevations on the map. What I meant was this: when I stand on two legs and let one bear my body's weight, they're not legs anymore. No longer two of the same thing. I didn't think about hanging myself until right this second, though there were ropes and beams above the bales and buckets, and the light made ladders up the walls.

[spool release]

My love, this afternoon the sky is mercury but so slow-moving. Berries have ripened in the thicket by the silo. Before all this began, I was the child beneath the table at a dinner that didn't end. Have I described to you my mother's Jacquard cloth? Gray ferns and snails on a rust red field. I tugged the border. I crawled on shoe leather. I was the leather inspector, and likewise inspector of hems and cuffs, heels and laces. Sometimes a hand reached down with piecrust. Now I sit on a broken wall of oval stones. The wall is like a chimney blasted from a house. Can a house produce its ruin—like its shadow—by a trick of time instead of light? I never came out between the chair legs. Glasses clink. Throats are clearing. Everything is blown apart.

Right on cue Ivor found the attic! A trunk of blanks from the Telegraph Office. The minimum charge is 20 words. We beg to advise, at the present writing, your letter has come to hand, awaiting your further commands, beg to remain. I fear boring our superiors with pro forma correspondence but hold out hope that brevity defends us. Did you know a question mark is a tone and not a stop? Another of the day's discoveries.

[spool release]

Our enemies are earnest! You should see them breaking cover, fleeing as we shoulder our potato guns. Among us Ivor is their only equal, scowling fiercely, face blacked but for the lips and livid eye, shooting fingerlings into the trees. Later, when he stormed the kitchen, threw down a sack of oyster mushrooms, I fried them with onions for his dinner while he hunched in the corner, steeling and buffing his knives.

[outstream]

Where do we live? It is to me at times in the shape of a town, in a collection of villages, and it is an open city. The fields are cleared from the burning, and the meadow baled and trim.

This shape is a chimera. The firestorm crosses the fields like any other storm, and trims the meadows to a flat horizon. We have only this last row of sheltering trees to break and redirect the flames. 'Trees like soldiers marching,' your ancestor wrote, in his most celebrated novel. He knew another war, another occupation. A half-dozen others.

What is a storm but a mechanical force? If only the trees could march. We once used the combine for threshing. Behold this ancient mechanism, which would so seek to separate us, for threshing, for thrashing, for crushing as fodder. A cause célèbere.

I should like very much to view your face on the screen, but those days are through. I have taken an oath of absolute and unconditional loyalty. But know this, if there is a rupture in the sound feed, it is a final boundary crossing, and a hidden transcript beneath the rehearsed story will suddenly begin to play. This is not a euphemism.

I was the resident commissioner. I engaged servants through the agency and the chauffeur I hired from within, a second son with a penchant for livery colors. He was driving in the motorcade when he exploded in the car. The bomb was small—granules stirred into his coffee—but with enormous yield, the blast size, by my calculations, more than sufficient to shatter glass and rip apart the metal, sending shrapnel into the pressing crowd. Imagine my surprise. The sound was soft. The metal held. The car stopped. The windshield wipers moved, but the windshield, coated on its inner face, could not be cleared. The driver's side window too had gone a plummy shade of black. Shortly afterward, when Carlotte delivered the rubber suit, I turned to neurotoxins with increased success. I knelt above my mistress who had run into the hallway as she died and kissed her through my mask. That is, I pressed my lips to the respirator that I pressed against her lips.

I can't go back to the city, even if I can find it, the buildings still standing, gutted but recognizable. The commander most likely made it to the blockhouse. I rolled over a hundred bodies, peeled back the lids, opened the mouths and checked the teeth against the records, filled pipettes. I couldn't get a positive ID on all I sampled but none of it was his.

Ivor nearly lost a thumb today. A snag in the mechanism of one of his beloved devices (he has sworn no oath against such things, but instead swears oaths and curses in his speeches which try the caretaker's sensibilities) and the board he so lovingly tooled upon the spindle struck back at him. Though the firm sofa is so fine for supporting ardent embraces and correct posture, it is rough terrain to cradle the head of an injured lad.

[spool release]

Certain collaborationists have founded a secret mail-opening service. Can you imagine! Mail! It actually bolsters me terrifically. It is the opinion of my voice, of my voice's memory.

[outstream]

How can you hear me, I speak from so far? You are lost between spirit and land, corporate and incorporate, floating in the tree limbs on the perimeter. And I did so admire your limbs! The battle is one of perseverance in this case. The cacophony which bore us up is now silent, and we must believe instead in alternating currents, such mysteries which have neither been penetrated nor dismantled, but encrypted, and coded for the duration.

I asked the caretaker if Ivor and I were family. I did not confess that I had already marked an almost irresistible force of attraction within the compound, making me cast aside every kind of duty, but to it alone. She consulted her manual of naming and deportment: though there is no such thing as family per se, she said, in this moment in history, we may call family a collection of humans grouped around us in the midst of distress. She directed my attention to a series of photographic plates illustrating the concept in lurid visceral detail.

To rent a room the papers must be in order. Travel permits, identity cards, letters of transit: scanable, encrypted, and enlaced with light pipes no thicker than a hair: personage and passage categorized in wave guides of reflected light in threads in the warp and weft. The papers are always a forgery. All identities are false. For them it's no matter of levity. The boarders are beginning to speak. Recitals by the gaslight, events logged in the recording spool, enumerated in the gazette. The stories they tell overlap. Annals which are non-concurrent, interims undefined, accounts of near approximates or distant integers. The stories do not add up.

Sequester and ride the rocking terrain, on compounds, in collectives, or remain always in transit, crossing and passing through increasingly regimented lines of resistance and patrol. If all the rotten eggs are collected in one basket, that will be the basket to watch. A brief show for the goons. To cross between checkpoints, papers must be in order, inspection and clearance, at frontiers and patrols or keep to the bushes, the hedgerows, the frames. Orders are insecure. The forgers have no idea what the documents look like. A march, or a line toward the margins, or skirting the rims, the trim verges, edges delineated only on future maps, contested even still, a shifting enclosure, a frayed hem, a contour, a fringe, the outliers. The borders are beginning to speak. They are always in transit, accounts of the distance between is arduous, and provinces stand in debate. The demarcation lines arbitrary—they do not follow any natural landmarks, but run haphazardly across departmental lines, even splitting some towns in two. The terrain of the occupied is shifting every day.

264R88

O POS

We sewed their entrails back into them and stood them up. Their nervous mechanisms enabled them to perform simple tasks—they could grip and swivel—but only in the yard. You see they ran on telluric currents. Inside the house, or wrapped as we were, in rubber and felt, they ceased to function. Some of us stripped off our layers and slept beside them on the dirt, reporting increased vigor. The vigor was channeled into the following: improved manual dexterity, better erections, sharper vision, more accurate thoughts. One barefoot woman who had adopted this regimen made it three-quarters of the way across the great lawn to the rostrum with four, then five, six, seven bullets in her body, before the eighth bullet, lodging in the thoracic spine, deactivated her limbs, so that she fell in the posture of one running against a wind, her knife arm drawn back, her fingers white around the handle. She could not signal to the arm, the fingers—Hurl! Release!—and lay motionless, a semiconductor on the drying grass.

351R00
O POS
REV

From glass tubes to stove pipes I have travelled along a road of lavender.
Once I was the switchman. Now, muddied paths, staunch partisans. There
are people, there are stories. The people think they shape the stories, but the
reverse is closer to the truth. Realms where the wearing of flesh is proscribed.
Amidst shrinking maids, gentlemen. I must not weaken, not now.

The worker priests are on the road. The bell of the last footpath. No evil,
no special blackness reserved for demons and monsters. Just this brotherless
one in his striplit mask.

What constitutes a lodger's city? How to build an imagined world on
the ruins of an occupied one. What details to include, what to invent to
take from the extant world, or the world which is passing. The various
manifestation of names, jealous names, a necessary confusion. The worker
priests, superimposed.

378L87

O NEG

I chased a wheeled horse through red sedges. It was a toy, controlled remotely, and I hoped it would lead me to the herd. Instead a woman was gesturing between the yellow boulders. She held her breast outside her shirt. She dragged me to the river and gripped my neck, sobbing. There was nothing to see. She said: what else could I have done with a basket so small? She repeated this several times. She seemed to have forgotten I had the power of speech and might answer her. For my part, I kept mum. I never again found the horse's trail.

[outstream]

Exchange the house for a sheltering boulder, the field for a trail blazed through briars. We can't be vagrant enough, legs rattling, as we leap the discarded bindles, leaving everything, even your handsomeness (I swear it wasn't that I was attached to) in our haste to escape from protocol. In school we wrote the slogan a thousand times: It is the Empire that gives us empirical bodies. I don't even know if I can touch you past this tree line. I don't know, in those days, when we wrote. There is always a remainder, what they meant for us. A happy future finishing the wounded? A way without doors?

[spool release]

Snow had fallen. In the village square, dogs rolled over and over. To call those impressions "angels"—did I do so knowing I made war on heaven? I waited a measure for the tape to roll before I answered: you will be pardoned. The caretaker threw down a leek and left the kitchen. The boarders moved their hands in buckets. Ivor pressed stop and I continued: you were innocent. Every star glittered between black frost and my blameless gaze.

195J60
A POS
MED

I'll share a mystery story with you, in shorthand. I came originally from Bistritz, of convoluted extraction which is rarely commented upon in these days, but which I still find notable in my profession. Most diseases run in the blood, even in the manufactured surrogate varieties. And I have often found my smattering of languages useful in field conditions, where despite all our wondrous technologies we are still married to the most rudimentary triage: use of dressing and ligature. Severance of limbs, of course, is preferable, if the proper prosthetics are available. I'm old-fashioned and prefer the carbon fiber and microprocessor models, especially when going above the knee. Less likely that their transmissions become crossed. Straight to the brain! Not a stealth jet mind you, but a jeep: it gets you there. Like a syringe for direct inter-human transfusion! If the blood is young it need not be defibrinated. I'll hook a lad to another lad and feed it straight, I'm not shy about these things. Were these not times of war, I'd be sacked. As it is, they're damn lucky to have anyone who knows how to work with the more arcane models and Dr. Agote's diluted solutions. I can make O Positive in a teacup out of almost any sanguine mélange.

They all cross my mind; I think of them often, that sea of limbs. There is hardly a foot of soil in this region which has not been enriched by the blood of men. And in the field, their lips are still gouts of fresh blood. They find it hard to look at one another in such conditions, I know that much. A youngster once begged for paroptic vision, to draw out the line of his aim. My boy, you are good to want an improved shot, but elective eyelessness! When corruption in the transit makes the goggles so scarce? And in the falling temperatures, a bit of ice on the piconet and the slave becomes the master! Do you want someone else seeing through your channels when you are stumbling blind in a trench? I think not.

I was firm, and told him he could not have it, whereupon he went without a word, gnawing at his fingers.

It may be the paprika which keeps me from sleeping, Leonie. I seem to see perfectly under my lashes. Again the operation. Again the narcotic. One more bag of fresh frozen plasma. Again some return of color to the ashy cheeks and then the regular breathing of healthy sleep. The flowers are of medicinal value and the breathing of their odor is part of the system of cure. My methods are always in question! Where one advances in a field of critiques one walks at all moments on something soft, flaccid.

A strong opiate tonight.

[outstream]

Nothing is given in advance. We study advents: the rabbit in the foliage, the book on the table that reappears and reappears and reappears.

123N56

A POS

The curfew bells rang at the oddest hours. I didn't always hear them. My wife, though, she was sensitive as fennel. I still see her as she was that morning, translucent in the street, shot through with scrutinies, resolutely projecting the image of a woman who had walked out alone from no place in particular, whose body was inclined to move any which way, who had never circumscribed her range of motion with attachment.

The house is none of its appearances. It is not the house the caretaker sees from within each tidied room. It is not the house I see from the barn or the enemy from the burning reeds across the field and from the biplanes. The house is the house seen from all possible perspectives. Ivor says this means the house is the house seen from nowhere in particular. That is why the enemy's planes circle endlessly, why the shots from the perimeter sail wide and wider. Ivor says we are invisible, by which he means we are safe for this moment. We should sleep.

789H00

B NEG

Simply to impress the Empress, the Mechanical Turk was procured by Surcouf, and so had been passed for years among the great houses and privateers of the port regions. In the traditional costume of turban and robes, perched across a long cabinet the Turk performed, in charming automation, *en passant* and the knight's tour with a vizier chess set in red ivory. In working the tour, from square to square a map could be managed by the steward, who was secretly one of the marshals of our local resistance militia! Voilà, stratagem exchanged to the insurgents! Following the map ensured safe transit to the brave girls with cropped hair, in trench coats and bobby socks, or onward to their leader, Nighthawk! O, how I long for those girls now.

But this is common knowledge. More interesting is the automaton himself, which when opened to the left, revealed clockwork, to the right, cogwork, opened front to back the gears penetrated the cabinet. Only pegboard and pantograph-style levers. It was a complicated design to mislead and confuse its patrons. Only after close inspection, and well knowing the nature of such devices, did I locate a shiftable panel, which did not conceal machinery, but a petite chamber with a silk cushion and a brass flagon of ale. There was no dwarf to fill the chamber! Instead a small girl from the western-most department of the peninsula: known for its megaliths and calvaires of stone crosses, you will know it well as a corsair stronghold. Their oil dialects are thought lost. Not so! As she executed the tour, from the safety of her cache, she spoke a trouvère lyric in the most lilting tones—one I know in my own high tongue, imagine!—in which a chevalier meets a lithe shepherdess who bests him in a battle of wits despite her demure demeanor. This chevalier— she sang his song not that of the shepherdess—ended his tale first in violent possession of the girl, next by beating a hasty retreat...

And this is how it happened in spring, how it happened in May
the wheat forms walls and the ground is moist
great labors sleep still under the frost
the hutches of my birds are empty
the wind cries in my chimney
look! the flowers recommence!
In the month of May after the hard winter...

This is how I knew it, or remembered it, in any case, in my own tongue, and so I told her as I leant into her cabinet.

As little rude as this might be, my little doe—I spoke to the girl in the automated Turk, Won't you come out of your cabinet and sit on my knee? I was so charmed by this ancient tune.

In my veins is the blood of old witches expelled from Scythia who mated with devils.

My kitten, you are too young to remember other than these warlike days. Blood was too precious a thing in that time of dishonorable peace...

My grandfather was a ship's captain, and he swore polyglot. I am from the corsair port.

My little badger, you are so devoted to your cause, you would sacrifice even those fine knickers I see at the brim of your waistcoat. Won't you come to bed with me? Even you must not work all night!

Listen carefully. I shall say this only once: Water sleeps and the enemy is sleepless.

And with that she shut her cabinet door to me.

It was at dawn that next morning when I heard the shattering burst of the war machines crossing the lines. Ten years! Ten years of infancy, sentimental, cruel and animal, disquiet, malaise, disorientation, all the penchant of impotence. I heard that Nighthawk's girls were all left for dead in a canal in their own village, on the island in the midst of three rivers, though I do not believe this. Too strong were their fields of desire.

[outstream]

Instead of coarse cotton, I dreamed I slept in a silk trap spun by spiders. Is it strange to dream of sleep, unabridged, webbed hours all around me? And of brightness, a leafless afternoon with sun on snow, a bomb with feathers floating overhead. Everything so quiet. The bomb unmoving, or buoyed slightly, now and then, by wind. It might have been a bird. A bubble of air in water, the white world washed by liquid in a lucent, back-lit globe.

The landscape is dormant. I don't hope for anything. Perhaps I am not yet awake. Getting out of bed my body was still leaning in to kiss you, and at the breakfast table, I did not eat, my hands taken up with asymptotal gestures.

[outstream]

We have our own chats on the rugs before the footed stove. On the inscription surface, a word only has meaning in use, the caretaker tells us. So much I already gathered. A difficult continuum: on the one hand a body in all its vulnerable nakedness, on the other hand a demonic grimoire of shortwave broadcasts of fireside chats, burning airships, mechanized invasions. The exchange of noise, sortable only by a certain focused derangement, toward meaning? Here was a moving mouth, the resonant ear, never the quiet hand, the reflective eye. No text this.

Does she mean on the body? Ivor asks. He is very literal and loathes the barbaric etchings on the skins of so many of our boarders. Affiliations. Alignments. Those are to denote systems of inclusion and exclusion. Scientific categories. I'm trying to talk about "in the days of the realm" the caretaker tells us. We are subjects of the realm. Only subjects are not substances, and therefore should be harder to displace with the drop of a stone. Or so I tell you from afar.

In the lodgers' common, a mural painting depicts scenes of rare and wonderful beauty: mountains, rivers, lakes, ocean, meadow, trees, flowers, winding roadways, sun kissed gardens—but with different coloring and vegetation. Depicted not through conventional means, but through recent means. The changing links between the locales and their medium.

The collared boarder begins the tale of his recent encampment. He says: The soldier priests were exiled or captured. Prisoner priests were provided with portable altars. Their conversations were with the dead: unpacking the thread. The community notes are of interest for the living, which I have thus recorded.

What? In writing? Ivor asked, bewildered. The boarder tapped his chest hatch fondly. Writing? he said, That storage monopoly? Hardly.

[outstream]

The caretaker wants to allow a flickering projection on the blackout cloth, once monthly, for the boarders. But I am not for it. It's enough for me that our own dead are projected in ambulation along the streets. However, I am reminded of those days when, working on the third floor of the house, you would project upon your large screen, and in full view of the windows, I could watch your entertainments from afar while I was coming down the meadow's steep slope.

I am a familiar of the cats! Ivor hurls at me from the crib. He knows about the dog I see in dreams and the store I set in her, an unfair advantage she offers me. How else am I expected to collapse space? I know I must close the gap between myself and my enemies. Face them on the same horizon line, not across it. Ivor hates it when I say such things, he insists that what we need is a proper vantage point. I do realize that by vantage point, he means he wants to see me from farther away.

422G54

AB NEG

Landlocked, now. No more the ship that carried a questioning glance from the crosshatches. Cormorant on her stern. Now simply a flag on the shore, a cloth lifted at the basin, on close inspection a needlepoint case, the inside velveteen, some lady's finery. I remember the days of the ladies. Now, except to rescue a captured comrade, you never let it be known that you exist. Names used to be given to the various sections of time. This was a day, etc. We are now approaching the instance in which death is most violent and life most clearly defined.

Which was the coming power? Was it a phalanx or a formalized front? Was it a band apart, avant-gardist and seducing? It retained many of the external trappings of the rise of the worst regimes: mass mobilization, discipline, indoctrination, physical fitness. Namely velocity. A group of relatively young technocrats within a single government. Political metaphor, such as commonly adopted by modern radicalized movements, costumed in their dark shorts.

A constant repetition of the same situations, the same thoughts and schemes. One lives and thinks in a nefarious coil. There is no progress, even time does not move forward in a straight line; it reappears in the same form.

Many marched the sedges. Adrift in the profligate field, the sight of the incarceration towers looming up out of the darkness, offered a sudden, if fleeting, comfort. They lifted a veil, and marked a linear course: release towards compass, and rampancy or straight to annihilation. Then, *passer à tabac*, the initial beating, the first of many. Fleeting, a moment of singular focus. The lenses aligned.

Girls and cafés are dangerous for more than one minute. I map. Ears hardened against images in the speech.

To write to you at length would lead to obsession.

From my post, I aimed and shot a figure breaking from the trees. I was jittery, having drunk a jar of Ivor's overdrawn tea—he boils oak bark in the kettle, pours that liquid on the leaves, and lets it steep; keeps our inner meats from rotting is his claim; he also packs his ears with salt—and shot too soon. It was one of the women, running zigzag in pursuit of cats. I took the citrons from her pockets and her clogs and stockings and her hair—what use had she for any of it? Besides, it was nothing more than protocol—but I felt, as I left her dismantled, sparking in the grass (no danger of conflagration; too swampy there for the field to catch), like the child I can't remember being, an orphan indifferent to caresses, pleased she had no one to answer to, only marks in the crowd.

769A23
A POS

They shaved the women on the hill behind the ministry, and while they shaved, the weather broke. You could say it was a storm. We dropped our pretenses and chased the knotted strands through parks. Wherever they caught on the tips of branches we gathered below, looking up, until a man cried out and fell onto his knees. Then those of us who'd kept our legs ran on.

Dictators are here again to be seen in power in this forgetful region, seen well by any who survives this epoch of obscured statements of relations, incommensurable variables. O accursed algebra!

The plane bounced upward. The unseen pilots had jettisoned their cargo and the night sky appeared as arboretum: plot, frame, flora, terrace, border, row. Then they pressed a brief flare to the underarm of the machine to show that it was all over. Nothing was left for us to do but collect the scattered treasure. Bright shiny avatars vying for affection among obviously analog people. Grayed avatars. I grayed them out.

[spool release]

How can you hear me? I speak from so far. The magister wind which has risen does not help matters. They say it is caused by the long and enclosed shape of our valley since the blasting of the plateaus. The mechanism is spooling again, assigning something to another device... As the hours go by my anxiety increases scarcely to be quieted even by the presence of the boarder Carlotte who is watching the road for passing convoys that might halt and attack us. Observe, report, set down the arithmetic of situations. Everyone is out at a task. I would like to look out at Carlotte, patrolling, and feel that there is another body close at hand. I would like to drag Ivor, half sleeping in tights and workshirt, into this bed—so unfair to conjure such a fear in you, though to imagine you occupied with my voice is to imagine your body in tact—and I have not slept without dram or draught for months, and this is the practice of duress, under siege. But, my love, my own one, the siege is commonplace, and much of our own making. I am forcing myself to picture you, in your narrow garb, in the high winds, even, in the wavering of branches where that dog is hovering. It is better not to talk to others about the dog, apart from Ivor. She materializes in the kitchen and I know it is wrong to try to touch her, but I often awake with the dream of having felt the solid form of the animal below her fur. Obviously, it's just a memory that I've held in the body, held from—

The mechanism has unearthed an historic scrap of voice from an ancient queue of data, and the spooler releases you back to me, over me: you're allowed to want me, but not to need me. Even to want you now appears crazed. But, O, pretty scraps from the past. Where retrograde, there is suspension, but a kind of sophisticated suspension.

I had been only 100 stokes in the bunker, when the pictographer reached us. He was a hesitant creature, a nervous man, ill-formed to his profession but he knew well the need for morale. Suddenly, there were seances and spirit photography in the anchored ballroom. The astrodome dropped down— providing an escape hatch—but could also be scrolled back to reveal the stars, a pathway for the transit of spectres.

We shared many nights together on the plane of the embrasure which pivoted and rotated but always remained floating on the surface of the dune. I longed to swim. Conversation was beyond me, but I was anxious to learn his trade. There seemed a living in it.

"Electro-optical lighting is the fruit of the recent technologies as much as those of the distant past.

The imagery comes about as the mirror image of a body that appears to be in terms of motor control more perfect than our own body," he told me. He was in mufti and leant against the side of the infrared column. "Never go unless you can do it in field boots and a helmet."

"A war of pictures and sounds is replacing the war of things, places," he said. He slid the cape onto his arms. The silence was unbroken; it grew closer and closer; it was thick, motionless.

He said, "I laid the very telephone cables which link us to the dead. Consider this: the human body consists of many infinitely thin layers of liquid ghost, that much we know. But if it is true that the spirit is created from nothingness, a 3-dimensional daguerreotype is a sinister trick despite the intricacy of its metal-working. It steals one layer after another until nothing remains of the spectres of the body. Photographs have always been the realm of the dead."

There will come a time when again there are nations. They will be strictly dependent on one another as organs of the same body. For now, there is only camouflage. If what is perceived is already lost, it becomes necessary to invest in concealment of those very things which once held power in their simple exploitation of one's available forces—for this reason our weapons are now ones of stealth, clouded in uncertainty. I count this as chimera. For in the realm of the real, everything begins with coldness, dizziness, and shortness of breath. And a word only has meaning through use.

We are building fences. Ivor says a fence is good. It keeps out the horizon. To reward me for my labors—I matched his pace; I didn't break for tea—he gave me a parchment charm. Remember once the world was full of them? No more. Loving would conduce to the failure of the mission. When Ivor looks up and says we see through glass and in an enigma he means you are never here in substance. I only saw you through your likeness. It is the same as saying, I say to Ivor, the stone I see is not within my eye. But walking to the house, I felt my lid catch upon an outcrop. I blinked until I bled. I feel it still—a hard small thing thrusting from the fibrous tunic like a boulder through the grass.

Of course they are also tunneling beneath us. When I walk in the yard the scurf sags beneath my feet, sways like a hammock. Inside the barn, between the slip and hay rake, I find an entrenching tool that I carry outside so I can squat with it across my knees looking down into the clovers. The clovers tremble constantly. They are tunneling closer and closer to the surface. The plants have little soil left to root in. When will they scrape too high, break through and reveal themselves? Particles of dirt are shaking loose, falling from beneath the mesh of grasses, falling upon the boring machines that they operate silently and that themselves are soundless, the cutting wheels spinning, the belts conveying muck, hauling our earth away, depositing it back behind the tree line.

[outstream]

What I mean to say is we have our pick of dangers. If each person is the unperceived term in the center of the world towards which all objects turn their faces then the absolute end can emanate from anywhere. Or we are all peripheral. In any case, it is almost over. Saturation is decreasing. There are short waves and long waves but I can no longer manipulate either. I spend hours looking through the window, blue sky, yellow field.

ID UNKNOWN

BLOOD UNKNOWN

Samizdat from the city of my birth tells its story. It was not destroyed but sealed beneath a dome of isinglass and aramid fibers. The worker priests allow one luxury: without fail, a cake baked with an extract that tastes of petrichor is presented to the nearest kin of the newly dead.

We exchange the roles of service, though so many nights I am the cook. The town is smaller and so targets stand out more clearly against the fields; and the population is obviously demoralized. The other waiters are gathered around the table discussing the last air raid and everyone's reaction to it; how Carlotte hid behind the table, Ivor gazed out a window, Hesslin stroked the hair of the donkey statuette, and the caretaker crossed herself fifty-seven times before she fainted. And she is no kind of believer. Incidentally, a false alarm.

I ask in whose hands our compound will fall this time?

Ours, says one of the former militiamen.

No, the rebels', says Howell.

Neither men are trusted among us. The porter looks at the star-lit sky and remarks: "Fine air-raid weather tonight. But what bridegroom will take us when we have lost all our limbs?"

[outstream]

We have a new pastime. We sit up of an evening in the kitchen and watch the stove by candlelight. Each of us wants to see the creature that is shitting in the skillet, its scat having produced no consensus as to species. Carlotte says mouse but Ivor pshaws this on behalf of his mousers and insists on bat. The boarder we have begun to call the Admiral mentions flying fish and, as you may expect, I guess vole and raise the wager by my favorite oddments, the bone-handled knife with oiled carbon blade and the walnut shell in the lines of which more than one beholder has claimed to see her father's face. No one trusts the others to keep watch and report faithfully, and so we pull our chairs into a ring and keep ourselves awake.

When we see it, I asked last night—by then it was almost morning, the tallow minutes dripping down—which of us will make the kill? A dozing boarder started and spoke.

We're already dead, he said half-muffled to the dark. Today, thinking of this moment, I tell myself the boarder could speak of his own forfeit only, that he had no right to speak for me, and I applied droplets below my eyes with the teat pipette to feel the moisture sliding toward my lips the way it once slid freely, do you remember? You touched it the last time you touched my face.

Howell begins the long saga. A bank of caves and grottos man-made, cut into solid cold rock by the first prisoners. Prison sounds are echo-less and bleak. A prisoner makes all sorts of laudable resolutions; he will do exercises every morning and learn a foreign language.

As he spoke the narrative, Howell watched the huge machine move ponderously through snow like a moving house. We were charged as an international case, he tells us. This is a phrase to mean a spy.

Into the inner grottos, and roughly fondled. There was no blast of firing from the cave, nor any movement. We passed through a double file of eyes — of wide-open, staring eyes, eyes without people attached to them. Eyes behind spyholes. We ran to the lip of the waste pit. A body, wrapped in a fur robe, was resting beside the well.

His colleague, who sat by the fire became animated in his chair. The flaxen-haired directress from an adjoining province also spoke up. Suddenly we all recalled the versions we had heard of this particular adventure.

Rap was her lover, said Hesslin, his voice was calm and matter of fact.
She hates Kiedron for killing him.
Kiedron didn't kill Rap; he suicided.
Arnie was in a coldsuit with a hood mike!

I fed a cube into the recorder, for you, my love. Ivor dozed. Kiedron clutched the handkerchief to his eyes. Hesslin slumped his head on the shoulder of the directress. He hoped someone had taken the time to hang his tunic and trimslax in a warm place.

Outdoors our posts are always empty. We harvest grapes and sometimes nap on bales despite the mildew that makes us cough. We haven't given up, but it's no good, the guarding, when the ground and sky are the enemies' embrasures. Better to ferment the must, better to lounge in last year's wheat, to sing with our mouths pressed to the necks of cats. Thrash in the elderbushes. Eat sunflower seeds. Put rosehips in the tea, and poppies. It's a different form of preparedness, a laxity that will allow us to sway with the shock waves, bend beneath the blades, open around the mortars and close up again like the surface of a long blue pond. Ivor says, Be gentle now. He plays horse; he plays hyacinth. He's soft to the touch and we follow his example.

[outstream]

What if you were implanted in my body? There are many things I can't remember and my skin is webbed with tissues grown over old punctures. I won't tell anyone this new hypothesis. I won't stop looking for you elsewhere. But so much would be explained if you were already here, interrupting the sensory-motor circuit—when my one hand grasps the other, the other hand grasping back.

Ivor was explaining virginity. What he said made sense, but now—

717J50

O POS

The savant and his conjecture is as follows. We struck out across the province in sunlit haze, the western meadows in a crystal globe.

At the rim of the outermost part, the loot of a hundred gitane caravans awaited us. A silk-walled tent hung with grid-worked tapestries and littered with rich carpets and velvet cushions. Dust-cast maidens, the obscure images from a hideous and half-remembered ambiguity. She-devils and sweet sisters.

Naught but diabolical cruelty of siege machines. Masters in their silvered mail. My monotype adversary on the horizon, and here we were together aiming pistols at the rows of cognate heads. I quartered an unshed tear.

It is an elevating thought that one should owe one's life to a set of dirty postcards, I told my savant.

I had often dreamt such a moment.

They'd gone to bed, Carlotte, the Admiral, Hesslin, Kiedron. To you they are names and don't need sleep. They doubtless flicker constantly, never more or less themselves. It is natural. I don't blame you. Do I flicker also? That is what I cannot bear—to be to you a call sign, a frequency that mingles with official broadcasts, a meshwork lover, more holes than anything. I shouldn't allow myself these fears. It is amazing—fear my greatest luxury. I have become so grand, with caches I will not open. We won't speak of it. What "we"? What "speak"? I am logging an event to make it happen. My love, I felt afraid confronted with unpeopled dark, the house in dormancy. The caretaker had left her wooden shoes and leather coat beside the fire. I walked the hall and felt the urge to tap on all the doors. Even the one with the empty bed behind it I could not bring myself to enter. I could not lie down. Some nights are like this. In the chair beside the kitchen window, Ivor slept away his watch. I shook him. He has the largest head. As it lolled to left and right, it rang. The tone was the tone of curfew bells. I felt in his hairline for a wire, probed inside his ears and mouth. The bells rang on and on. I thought of the barefoot woman twitching on the lawn, the hair of the collaborators, how it snagged on twigs and thorns and tree bark, bricks and iron. You pulled a wheeled horse through sedges red with blood and I chased after. I wanted to photograph you naked by the river, to print a dirty postcard of your limbs in grapple with my own, to print this postcard a thousand times and translate the image into a matrix of lights and darks, something we could project onto the bottom layer of the clouds and stand under, open mouthed, awaiting death most violent, seeing life most clearly defined.

Every man awaits his murderer. Or else a shepherd to appear, unarmed but sly, aware of tree-obscured defiles that lead to cliffs and caves. Ivor swears he hid L-pills in the pantry in a jar he'd labeled peas. It's not there but he will not change his story. He swigs from a brass flagon and, swallowing, passes neither left nor right but tucks it back inside his coat.

333J95

AB NEG

Colm and I flew forty-odd missions, dropped leaflets and bomblets, miniaturized the city then swooped low to strafe the fields. On the returns, flying through the dark, cold in my jacket, surrounded by the smoke of Colm's cigars, I listened for the beacons and dreamed of planes with astrolobes, moonlight streaming down through glass to play on the controls. I wanted to gaze up through the cabin roof to navigate by star and sextant. My father was a sailor. He died young and to my knowledge never killed anything human. I have no knowledge of what has died beneath me. When the fire jumped from wing to fuselage I watched Colm strapped and burning shoot up into the air beside me, but I don't know more than that.

[outstream]

No contact outside the network. But I must love you, even if it does me violence. The words they will force from me through tortures, I give you freely. Little fox of the hollow trees, of the moon craters, withdraw into darker gulfs, the whole place is for another. There is no future left on earth. The siren is sounding. It's a martyr's bell. It's an executioner's whistle. I am sealed in, a fish in a frozen lake. The ripples I made are solids — orbs, ladders, blue and green petals — and I see your paw prints in the frost above, my hope, escaping. I will signal to the last, beyond the last. It might be over. This signal might well have come from no one.

Our enemy is upon us. I cover lightbulbs with mud. The caretaker melts the cutlery. She would rather drink hot silver than allow a man in a hat to touch her spoons. Be assured of our existence once and for all. Each present permanently underpins a point in time. Ivor will be then and now as always turning leeks in a bucket of cold water. The twisted paper is unlit in the hearth. I can already see the meadow all around me as though every wall is gone.

Ivor claims it's not the end but its congener. The Admiral agrees. He made his career out of exactly this. If I say, Look through the wall, the world's on fire; the Admiral points up to the clouds, says, Look at the canvas and cordage untouched by the lightning. But the smell of cooking meat and scorched corn? The boarders' screams?

I insist: They're here, the ardent killers of real beings.

Which one of us is real? asks Ivor, laughing. That one should run. The rest will hold them.

Return to the front? Define front, I defy you. There is nothing in the tenets of even the most tenebrous monastic order which condemns a man to endure purgatory, and then, when it is all over, sends him back to the mouth of Gehenna. No, we began the exode. A dramatic but temporary demographic.

Our cultural vestiges have been outlawed! I know this; I was once a photographer. I kept that grim task still in the prison encampment. Look here, at this memento. I took this photo myself. Note the makeshift posts, in just the first months after the initial surrender. Comrades slumped against their wrist bindings, blindfolded, before the firing squad in their rough mountain garb. The appeal is to the ear, not the eye, which perishes.

Still more often I dream that I must return to encampment No. 41 because I have left something behind there. The spoken symbol formed by means of various organs in or about the mouth. The internee changes form and color, and assumes the cast that most easily enables him to secure a maximum of those minimal advantages possible within the framing.

The image of execution, encaptured in the lens, at first glance appears illogical. It is no longer, in this era, limited by the duration of ink, paper, observers, as it once was against the duration of flesh, blood, and the body. It is recorded without material trace.

[spool release]

You need me to be locatable, to receive your signals, to gather this space and make a site exist. Interpret my silence as condolences, the static as reception.

[outstream]

I had hoped—a granary outside the postern, trees made of wood, grasses with stalks yellow and less yellow, unseen squirrels, barn-shaped scent of hay and raisins, groundwater freezing, thawing, hutches, a house, long table to sit around, distance from the center become at last partition, something behind which to shelter. Mushrooms growing in that shaded margin to pick white and pickle. I had hoped at most it was a place. Not miraculous—the mutilated with phantom legs dense enough to dance on; melodies audible to everyone—only forgotten, on the wayside of even wayside flowers. I could summon you and the signal would not return. I could love you safely. I could look around and want to see you because absolutely you aren't here.

Retrieve the torso blown into the chestnut tree. Check it against the heads. One head is distinguished from the others by a patch fastened to the eye. In red thread stitched into the silk four letters: *voir.*

Is there a sign of political alignment? No, the signs were wireless, went to air. Look for an archive in vapors rising from wet ground. What scale of notes would make it open? The insurgents stippled ether. They made absence the conveyance. Others plowed the field and sowed their cables. They never hoped for life under a fixed regime but as the *relationship between phenomena.* They desired speed in correspondence.

Information is camouflaged. It has become identical with the scene itself— twisted metal, corpses, pitted earth, bricks, glass, mud, canvas—and so has disappeared.

They died in action, in real-time, in this diorama of their making. Terrorists. Anarchists. Strategists. Illusionists. They played games with duration and delay. Compress the space via aerial perspective. Zero out. Eliminate the territory. The boundaries converge at the vanishing point. Under a camera eye they performed their parts, moved between structures, posed, were things to be seen. Meanwhile, language, bodiless, emitted without origin or end.

They cancelled out reality. They erected blinds, reflective or matte surfaces, fences, screens that scrolled clouds or water. They represented nothing, imitated nothing, corroborated nothing. They were nothing's collaborators inhabiting sham landscapes. Accelerating within the spot as though to break a barrier, cross into another world. There are iron hatches in the turf of the perimeter. One center of operations—whose?—was constructed underneath.

Inspect the limbs and organs, the prostheses. There are motors inside half the heads, indissociable from the bony plates, riveted by skilled technicians, factory trained. The corn crib is filled with metal salvage. From the fraying in the lining of the torsos, it can be determined that they ingested chemicals, composition as yet unknown, cause of ingestion unknown, effect of ingestion unknown. The dominant odors in the surveyed area: humus, niter, ozone, petrol, latex, iron.

The floodplain is saturated with bloods, all types, to be pumped and treated, stored in mobile units and trucked to the phalanstère. Blood is still in short supply. In the beginning, no one knew how to miss the feeling of that fluid movement, a sensation unperceived, but then they learned. The priests in kiosks at the points of sale mix and remediate the kilos to make a general formula. This liquid, priced dear in its bag, with its coil of transparent tube, is fit for any valid person, all those who come with permits, paper monies, nostalgia for the living.

"The enemy! Simultaneously! All sectors!" we chant as a sort of prost over the herbal liqueurs. Gleefully Kiedron showed us all his treasures: a machine gun *à l'annciene* (we each of us had to fire off a few rounds), his alloy horses (two of them were led right into living room where we were having our meal and they sniffed at the dish of mutton), and a chest full of detonating pomegranates (we were invited out of politeness to throw one, but we refused with thanks).

The hostelry guests this night are mainly pilots.

.

I climbed the fence. I struck out across the province in a sunlit haze. I had to crawl along the verges while the caravans made a silk horizon, a ribbon of heliotrope and silver, then I ran into the trees, slid into the canal, walked in water between the earthen walls, slept standing with my brow against a pylon, and woke to the barking of the dogs my dream ranged hungry on the lower bridge. Be brave! I won't crawl now. I won't stop running. If I can reach and activate the turbine, I can aim the death beam all around me, I can shoot in each direction, I can make of every side a sheet of fire. I left you eyeless at your post, bleeding wrists, black blindfold. I left you with an L-pill in your mouth in your molar made of quartz. You want to bite and be absorbed by flame, and in that oscillation, to generate the signal. Do it. It's almost time. I will record you. Without howling or feedback. Clear as day. A recording without material trace.

Journeys end in opened fire. Journeys end at the merciless parliament. Journeys end in the trench at the foot of the wall. Journeys end in the residuum of the counter-insurgency in the lovers reaching through the wires with fingers stiffened into claws. Journeys end in autumn songs. The field is cold. Tonight the centerpiece will be bouquets of sticks. Carriages return. The feed line prefers radishes for dinner. Those seeds are from the Judas Tree. Ivor loves verveine. The parsnips have withered. How strange the soup is dry and black. How strange the pigeons fill the chimney. Journeys end in time. The simple flowers of our spring are what I want to see again. Journeys end in undergrowth in berries underfoot. Journeys end when the metaphorical becomes the current sense. Disaster that fails finally to fall short of the absolute disaster that annuls it.

Long ago, we wrote only as a complement to speaking. Text a coherent set of symbols in transmission, text an arrangement, a function of memory, which comes to a surface. Text is anything that can be read. This was long ago and quite far away, with skies overcast, when what we wrote and what we spoke diverged. And what we spoke and what we spoke diverged. A parting of dialects. Write it down: the highly codified languages of the formal, the particular, the specific, but never the ordinary. Speech in transcription. These are not corruptions of the high variants, but operating on a continuum. This was long ago.

Occupation drips. But now the messages have been sent and the voices in flux, the lines direct and indirect, the passage noted, the thought recorded, the ghost in the sound booth collects all the tracks, and sound is captured more clearly now, anywhere, if the room is small, if the walls secure. And then stitched, patched, sampled, and corrupted, in loops, and in streams.

Finally, I beg you, a scrap of your voice and what then? Winter in the column of my hind parts! The djinn's gaslight is mine! Bygone the doleful sidereal, the diurnal course, the extent, the orbit, the epoch! Span and term, continuance a shamrock! Mistresses distresses now through. Fishes of long ago come true.

And so I sign off. In clover. In olives. In lavender oil. In a hovel. In mountain vales. In lava floes, in volcanoes. In vernacular prose. In novels. With wolves. Devolve. Dissolve.

Don't protest. I am not within harm's reach. I am the harm itself. Don't close the distance I open with each attempt at contact. This architecture is the shape the ambush takes when time has stopped. I am inside. Don't believe me. It's a trap. I am. Yours in haste.

Joanna Howard lives and works in Rhode Island.

Joanna Ruocco is a writer who lives and works in North Carolina.

ACKNOWLEDGMENTS

We would like to thank the *Brooklyn Rail*, and in particular Rita Bullwinkel and Donald Breckenridge for publishing an excerpt from *Field Glass*. Thanks as well to Kate Schapira and Hollis Mickey and the RISD Art Museum for inviting us to stage and perform scenes from *Field Glass*. Thanks to John Cayley for audio and video collaboration, and some incomparable voice acting, and to Dr. David Penn for his audio recording of this performance.

Further thanks to Thangam Ravindranathan, Andrew Colarusso, and Renee Gladman for the generous support, enthusiasm and words of encouragement around this project.

Field Glass is deeply indebted to the poetic war journals of Rene Char, *Leaves of Hypnos*, also to Paul Virilio's *Bunker Archeology*.

The two of us wrote *Field Glass* together. Since each of us was several, there was already quite a crowd. Here we have made use of everything that came within range, what was closest as well as farthest away.

SIDEBROW BOOKS | www.sidebrow.net

ON WONDERLAND
& WASTE
Sandy Florian
Collages by Alexis Anne Mackenzie
SB002 | ISBN: 0-9814975-1-9

BEYOND THIS POINT
ARE MONSTERS
Roxanne Carter
SB009 | ISBN: 0-9814975-8-6

SELENOGRAPHY
Joshua Marie Wilkinson
Polaroids by Tim Rutili
SB003 | ISBN: 0-9814975-2-7

THE COURIER'S
ARCHIVE & HYMNAL
Joshua Marie Wilkinson
SB010 | ISBN: 0-9814975-9-4

NONE OF THIS IS REAL
Miranda Mellis
SB005 | ISBN: 0-9814975-4-3

FOR ANOTHER
WRITING BACK
Elaine Bleakney
SB011 | ISBN: 1-940090-00-8

LETTERS TO
KELLY CLARKSON
Julia Bloch
SB007 | ISBN: 0-9814975-6-X

THE VOLTA BOOK OF POETS
A constellation of the most innovative
poetry evolving today, featuring 50 poets of
disparate backgrounds and traditions
SB012 | ISBN: 1-940090-01-6

SPED
Teresa K. Miller
SB008 | ISBN: 0-9814975-7-8

IN AN I
Popahna Brandes
SB013 | ISBN: 1-940090-02-4

VALLEY FEVER
Julia Bloch
SB014 | ISBN: 1-940090-03-2

THE YESTERDAY PROJECT
Ben Doller & Sandra Doller
SB015 | ISBN: 1-940090-04-0

THE WINE-DARK SEA
Mathias Svalina
SB016 | ISBN: 1-940090-05-9

INHERIT
Ginger Ko
SB018 | ISBN: 1-940090-07-5

To order, and to view our entire catalog, including new and forthcoming titles, visit www.sidebrow.net/books.